SINK OR SWIM

SINK OR SWIM

Tash McAdam

orca soundings

ORCA BOOK PUBLISHERS

Published in Canada and the United States in 2021 by Orca Book Publishers.
orcabook.com

Library and Archives Canada Cataloguing in Publication
Title: Sink or swim / Tash McAdam.
Names: McAdam, Tash, author.
Series: Orca soundings.
Description: Series statement: Orca soundings
Identifiers: Canadiana (print) 2021009513X | Canadiana (ebook) 20210095156 |
ISBN 9781459828513 (softcover) | ISBN 9781459828520 (PDF) | ISBN 9781459828537 (EPUB)
Classification: LCC PS8626.C33 S56 2021 | DDC jc813/.6—dc23

Library of Congress Control Number: 2020951468

Summary: In this high-interest accessible novel for teen readers,
trans teen Bass and his girlfriend, Rosie, have to battle the elements to survive.

Orca Book Publishers is committed to reducing the consumption
of nonrenewable resources in the making of our books. We make
every effort to use materials that support a sustainable future.

Orca Book Publishers gratefully acknowledges the support for its
publishing programs provided by the following agencies: the Government
of Canada, the Canada Council for the Arts and the Province of British
Columbia through the BC Arts Council and the Book Publishing Tax Credit.

Edited by Tanya Trafford
Design by Ella Collier
Cover photography by Stocksy.com/Mark Windom (front) and
Shutterstock.com/Krasovski Dmitri (back)

Printed and bound in Canada.

24 23 22 21 • 1 2 3 4

*For all the youth at the Gender
Generations Project (formerly known
as the Trans Tipping Point):
You amaze me.*

Chapter One

It's a beautiful day for a first date. The sky is a clear blue almost all the way to the horizon. Far in the distance, dark clouds cover the mountains. Past the shoreline waves, the ocean is as smooth as silk. Bass slips for the third time as his old sneakers hit a wet patch of seaweed. He skids and almost drops his end of the heavy boat he and Rosie are carrying. Cursing, he tries to ignore the view and concentrates on putting one foot in front of the other. Only ten yards to the water. He can make it, even if his fingers do feel like they're about to be ripped off. Sweat runs down his face, stinging his eyes. His multicolored hair is plastered to his forehead. *Bet I look great*, he thinks sadly. On the bright side, it's always windy on the coast, so Rosie already knows what he looks like with a mop on his head.

"Take a deep breath, Bass. You look like you're about to collapse," Rosie says. She lets go of the boat with her right hand to sweep her fringe out of her eyes. Of course, she can hold the boat with one hand. She's stronger than Bass, even if he's much bigger. Her strength comes from all the time she spends climbing and throwing heavy metal things around. She's one of the best hammer throwers in the province. Bass's favorite sports are all played with a controller and a headset. Online gaming is not so great for building up your biceps.

Bass nods and inhales deeply. A deep breath of ocean air fills his lungs and helps settle his nervous stomach. His feet slip again on the slimy seaweed coating the smooth rocks, but he doesn't fall. Rosie grins at him, her round face glowing with excitement.

"This is going to be great! No one will even notice we're gone. You know Old Jack never takes this boat out anymore. I steal it all the time!" Rosie fist pumps and then grabs the crusty rope tied to the front of the old wooden boat again.

"I know." Bass tries hard to believe her, but the voice in his head won't be quiet. *You'll get caught! You'll get expelled for skipping school. Rosie will get bored once she's stuck with you all day and finds out how annoying you are, and then she'll dump you. You'll fall overboard and drown.* For a kid who grew up on an island, Bass is embarrassingly scared of the ocean. And all the stuff that lives in it. As well as animals. And girls. Most things, really. His counselor has told him it's anxiety, and that it's manageable, but Bass just feels like a loser.

Bass slip-slides forward. He's tugged along by Rosie as she strides confidently toward the foaming sealine. With one last glance back, Bass pushes the inner voice down and concentrates on not falling over. That would not be a great start to their first real date. Sharing lunch at the Pride Club meetings doesn't count as dating.

In the small cove behind them, a large brown tarp looks like it still hides a boat. But all that's under there now are their abandoned schoolbooks and Bass's backpack. Rosie's pack is wedged into the small boat locker and stuffed with sandwiches and drinks. Honestly, Bass is really looking forward to the sandwiches. He's hot and tired already, and the day has barely started. It must be close to ninety degrees right now, and the air is muggy and still. He tries to distract himself from the great weight of the boat by thinking about how cool Rosie is. He still can't believe that she somehow wants to spend the day with him. She's got incredible fashion sense, she's good at sports, she's a straight-A student, and everyone likes her. Bass is a C-minus kind of guy at everything, including life. His counselor has told him he should try to banish the negative self-talk, but it's so hard.

Bass jumps in surprise when water splashes up over his shoes, wetting him to mid calf. The sharp smells of brine and fish fill his nose. Together, he and Rosie guide the boat down into the shallow water. The smile Rosie gives him as she hops into the boat shows off all her dimples. It puts a warm feeling in Bass's belly that finally lets him relax. When he grins back at her, Rosie crinkles her nose at him. She's adorable.

"You need to relax, Bass," she says. "This is going to be great."

"I'm trying," he replies. The boat bobs up and down, making it more difficult to get in. Determined, Bass pushes the boat forward. It glides into deeper water almost too fast for him. He hurls himself over the gunwale and tumbles into a heap in the bottom of the small boat. Rosie laughs as water splashes over the side after him. Spluttering on a mouthful of the ocean, Bass grabs the transom and pulls himself into a sitting position.

"All this suffering is going to be worth it when you see my private bay," Rosie says. "It's so special, Bass. I promise you're going to love it."

The sunlight catches her hair, turning the dark waves red and copper. Her brown eyes dance with mischief. She looks happy and free and, for some reason, glad that Bass is with her.

He can't help but smile back at her, squinting into the sun. "It's already worth it," he says. He's surprised to find he actually means it. Rosie winks at him and moves down the boat. She fiddles with the old outboard motor for a few minutes while Bass tries to get comfortable. By the time the motor is down and churning the water into creamy waves, Bass has found a secure position on the central bench.

Ahead of them, the ocean spills out, huge and so blue it almost hurts to look at it. An eagle screams and hurtles across the sky, making Bass jump and Rosie giggle. "I'm going to teach you to appreciate our beautiful islands today if it kills us both," she says, wagging a finger at him. "Now, cabin boy. Fetch me some juice."

Chapter Two

Bass rolls his eyes at Rosie but uses his foot to nudge the locker set into the bow of the boat. It sticks a bit, and he notices pale blue paint flaking off and settling in the wash of water at the bottom of the boat. It seems like more water than he could have brought in with his awkward entrance.

"Uh, Rosie?" he says. The water pooling at the bottom of the boat is rippling. "Rosie!"

"What? Where's my juice?" Rosie asks. She turns back and looks at him.

"I think we have a problem," Bass says, trying to sound calm. He is not sure he succeeds. The voice in his head starts up again.

The boat is leaking—you're going to sink!

You'll drown out here and no one will ever find your bodies.

Your shoes will wash up on the shore like that kid who fell overboard last year.

The fish are going to eat your guts.

Fear makes his fingers clumsy as he leans down to feel around in the puddle of water. He can feel a gap about as large as his thumb between two of the planks. Pale wood stands out against the faded old paint. A huge splinter must have broken off, leaving the hole. Panic fills him, and his breathing gets short and choppy. The whine of the engine throbs in his ears. But then it abruptly stops.

Rosie splashes down into the bottom of the boat and tugs on his earlobe with warm fingers until he looks at her. "Bass. Bass! It's okay! These old boats spring little leaks all the time. Everything's fine. We'll patch it up. We can bail the water out. We won't sink. We won't even have to turn around!"

"Of course we have to turn around!" Bass wishes his voice didn't sound so high-pitched. The tape binding his chest flat suddenly feels itchy and too tight. "We're…sinking…" His words break up. He tries to breathe like his counselor told him to. *Slow and steady, in for four, hold your breath. Breathe out for four, hold your breath.*

"We're okay. I promise. Look, I'm going to block it up right now." Rosie speaks calmly, her nimble fingers making a knot out of some rope and stuffing it into the small gap. The water shoves at the blockage, still squeezing past but more slowly. And then the ripples calm, the gap mostly filled. Rosie darts in and kisses Bass on the cheek. "See!"

She sounds so sure of herself. Bass manages to get a full breath into his lungs, and that helps a lot. Slowly the fear drains away. Feeling stupid and embarrassed, he busies himself reaching into the half-open locker. He thinks about that spontaneous kiss on his cheek.

"Let me get your juice," he says, fumbling with the bag. When he pulls it out, he blinks, confused. It's his gray backpack. But the food isn't in *his* backpack. It's in Rosie's. Bass reaches into the locker and fumbles around, desperately hoping to find the other bag.

"Oh no." Bass swallows, trying to figure out what happened. After he'd repacked the bags, Rosie had sent him down to the rocks while she arranged the tarp to look like the boat was still there. Bass's job was to watch the beach for anyone coming along who might object to them taking the boat. She had yelled, "Which bag did you put the shit in?" and he'd yelled back "Mine!" Oh. *Way to go, Einstein.* When

Rosie said "shit," she meant food. But Bass had thought she meant their school shit. Sandwiches aren't shit. Obviously. Sandwiches are delicious.

Frowning, Rosie grabs the backpack and pulls out Bass's Socials textbook. "Oh. Wrong bag," she says.

She's quiet for a moment, and Bass can't bear to look at her face. He knows it's going to tell him he has ruined their picnic before it's even started. An anxiety attack before they're even clear of the bay, and getting the bags mixed up to boot. Then a warm shoulder thumps into his.

"Oh my god, you look like someone just caught you murdering a baby seal," Rosie says, laughing. "It's fine. We can go to the beach for an hour and then come back when we get too thirsty."

"I'm such a loser," Bass says, frowning at his shoes. His body feels hot with embarrassment.

"A cute loser." Rosie nudges him with her shoulder again and clambers back up to restart the engine.

Bass has noticed that Rosie touches him a lot. More than anyone except his mom, really. He feels the heat spread over his whole chest, up past his collarbones and into his cheeks. He doesn't get called cute very often. His mom used to call him cute, back when he went by the name Elizabeth and everyone thought he was a girl. Since he has come out, she overcompensates. He's always her "strapping young lad" and "handsome boy." It's nice, but…nowhere near accurate. Bass is not entirely sure what "strapping" really means, but if it's big and strong, well, nope. And handsome doesn't work either. Cute, said with the warmth that Rosie used, he can kind of believe. He could be cute.

Feeling better than he has all day, Bass busies himself bailing out some of the sloshing water with a handy bucket. The sun beating down on his head—he definitely should have worn a hat—feels friendlier all of a sudden. The wind whipping his hair against his cheeks feels fresh and promising.

Even the choppy motion of the waves bouncing under the hull of the boat seems fun and exciting instead of scary and sickening. He notices the dark clouds gathering above the distant mountains. But right here, right now, the weather, and the company, is perfect. The rocky island they're heading toward is getting bigger. They'll be there soon, and he'll get to spend as much time as he wants with Rosie. Well, maybe not as much time as he would have if they'd brought food and water. But some. And no one will be able to listen to their conversations or point and stare. Perfect.

Chapter Three

It happens so fast, Bass can't make sense of it. One minute the sun is streaming over them, and the next, a huge cloud blocks out its rays. The wind picks up enough that whitecaps slam into the sides of the boat, rocking it hard. Bass loses his balance. He catches himself on the side of the boat and spins around to look at Rosie. What he sees doesn't fill him with confidence. Before, Rosie's wide mouth .

was laughing and happy, but now it's tight and small. She's frowning in concentration, steering them through the growing waves in a large circle, trying to turn them around.

"Rosie..." Bass doesn't really know what to say.

"Yeah, I got it. Put your life jacket on," she says, clearly distracted.

"What else can I do?" Bass tries to sound brave, like the oncoming storm isn't scaring him at all. The sky has turned an ugly dark color, like a bruise. It's like the sun was never there. Bass has lived on the coast his whole life but has never seen a storm roll in this fast. Rain suddenly pours down, drenching him from head to foot. His sun-warmed skin prickles and tightens in the cold. He struggles into his life jacket and pushes Rosie's over to her. She drags it over her head in a couple of quick, practiced movements.

"Bail!" Rosie yells over the noise of wind and waves. Water is slopping over the edge of the boat, and the size of the pool in the bottom is growing rapidly. Bass's shoes squelch as he moves as quickly as he can to grab the pail.

Throwing water over the side is a good distraction. Scoop, throw. Scoop, throw. He can do that. Repetitive, mindless tasks are his specialty.

The boat struggles against the angry ocean. Waves tall enough to fill the boat and swamp them crash past on either side as Rosie expertly steers them through the gale.

"We're not going to make it back!" she yells over the waves. "I'm going to take us in to land on my beach. We can wait out the storm there."

Cold fear has settled in Bass's bones, making his reactions slow and his hands stupid. But he keeps bailing. The bucket slips in his hand as he leans out to empty it. The rough metal lip around the edge catches and slices his index finger. He yells out in pain but doesn't drop the bucket. He leans out over the side of the boat as he tries to get a better grip.

Salt water bashes into his side, drenching him. The force of the wave hitting him is enough to shift his weight. Leaning dangerously far out now, Bass loses his balance. He feels the moment when it's too late. As he tumbles overboard, water jumps up to meet him, slapping him in the face and pushing into his nose. He flails his arms in one last desperate attempt to save himself.

A strong hand grabs him by the back of his shirt and hauls him back in. Rosie throws them both down in the bottom of the boat. Coughing up salt water and puke, Bass tries to sit up. Rosie grabs his shoulder and pulls him back down, crawling close enough to yell in his ear over the noise.

"Motor's gone, and the oars too. Stay down. I'll try to bail," she says. Her face appears brave and confident, but even through the lashing rain Bass can see the fear in her eyes. She doesn't let go of him, holding on to his shoulder like an anchor. Bass is surprised when he realizes his freezing fingers are still clutching the metal pail. Rosie takes it from him. Shivering and miserable, they huddle together. Bass grips Rosie's hips as she makes a useless effort to bail out the boat. It's clear that she can't get rid of enough water to make a difference.

"It's going to sink," Bass says and tugs her back down. At least they can be together when it happens. Rosie turns to look at him, and her face crumples into tears.

"I'm sorry!" she says.

"It's not your fault," he replies. It's almost impossible to hear each other over the storm. The waves keep thundering down onto the boat, splashing water over them.

"I should have checked the weather report!" Rosie hides her face in Bass's neck, curling her fingers into the shoulder straps of his life jacket. "If the boat flips over, we can use it to help us float. But if we're washed up onto the rocks, let go. It'll get smashed to pieces."

"Weather report said blue skies all day." Seeing Rosie looking so terrified inspires Bass to be brave, comforting. He puts his arms around Rosie and holds her. It feels right. He's surprised he's not a crying mess, but somehow right now he's not feeling any anxiety. Just normal, gut-squeezing terror.

The wave that finally floods the boat completely isn't any bigger than the earlier waves. It just hits at the perfect angle. The wall of water breaks on top of them, and the boat flips. Everything rushes past too fast to even think about. Bass breathes water, air, water. Rosie is snatched out of his arms as if a giant had grabbed her. Then Bass is completely underwater. The sudden drop in sound is the most surprising part. He's already soaked to the skin, so actually being in the ocean doesn't feel too different for a moment. But the roaring wind and crashing water sounds are muted. His life jacket pulls him to the surface. Coughing and thrashing, Bass kicks his shoes off and tries to turn around.

But "around" has no meaning now. Everything is water. Above him, below him, around him. Water is the only thing, gray, black and blue. The rain is so heavy he can't see through it. Where is Rosie? Where's the boat? He's drowning on the surface of the ocean, bobbing around helplessly in the huge waves. Rain streams down his face, water splashes into his mouth. He can't breathe.

Chapter Four

Through a gap in the waves, Bass sees a flash of something pale. The boat or Rosie! It has to be one of them. Determination flows back through him, and he shields his mouth with his hands so he can take two, three, four gasping breaths. Filling his lungs pushes the panic down. He gets himself under control and flips onto his back. Once he's sure he won't roll over, he starts kicking, hoping that whatever he saw is still in this direction.

Fighting against the water is impossible. The best he can do is let the waves pull and push him in a zigzag toward his target. Time stretches out and becomes an awful blur of kick, roll, kick, roll. He chokes again and again, feeling the cold take his strength. Even moving his feet is more than he can manage. The ocean bullies him, forcing its way up his nose and down his throat. His lungs are burning. He can't get enough air. It's so cold, he can't feel his arms or legs anymore. This is it, he knows. Even with the life jacket keeping him afloat, he'll drown soon. He's so tired he can't move. He looks up at the pouring gray rain above him and waits to die.

Suddenly he spins around. Something's caught his foot! Was it a shark? Even though he knows the waters here are far too cold for that to be likely, the thought of being eaten alive delivers a last rush of energy. That and panic give him the strength to kick out desperately. His numb foot whacks something hard. He cries out in terror, doubling his effort to swim away from whatever is hunting him.

His back smashes into something too hard to be water. Whimpering in fear, Bass closes his eyes, not wanting to see death. I'm sorry, Mom, he thinks. A wave whisks him up and dumps him down. All around him, water drains away. He feels the cold wind on his stomach under the life jacket. He's on top of something, out of the water. Opening his eyes, he expects to see an ugly monster. A shark hunting him, or something even worse. But instead he sees barnacles. A rock! Elated, he tries to sit up, only to be thrown clear by another crashing wave. But rocks mean land, safety! With the last of his strength, Bass reaches for the rock. Then something whacks him in the head, and everything goes dark.

Pain. A lot of it. Bass's right arm hurts so much. Feels like it's burning. His head pounds. He can feel his heartbeat in his ears and throat, even in his tongue, which is fat and dry and stuck to the roof of his mouth. Weakly Bass flaps his arm over his body, trying to move away from the source of heat. There's a weird squawking sound. His eyes won't open. They're stuck together, the sand and salt and crusted tears like glue. It takes him a moment to realize he's alive. That doesn't make any sense. He remembers being in the water. Dying. He remembers a shark…no. It wasn't a shark, it was a rock. He was washed up onto a rock. Then he hit his head.

His arm flares with pain again. Something's very wrong. With his good hand he reaches up to wipe his eyes. They hurt too. Everything hurts. His head feels swollen and heavy. Finally he manages to open his eyes, just as another blast of pain hits his arm.

A seagull is perching on his life jacket, eyeing him. Oh, that explains the squawking. The bird pecks at the bloody cut on his forearm again.

Bass yells. The sound comes out broken and dry, but it's enough to scare the awful bird away. It flaps into the sky with a bloody strip of Bass's skin in its beak. Bass retches, and liquid dribbles down his chin and chest. It's mostly seawater, and it stings his throat and dry mouth.

Scraping himself off the ground takes a while. The storm is still raging. Bass manages to get himself into a sitting position. Carefully he touches the back of his head with his fingers. There's a big, hot bump. When he pulls his hand back, blood shines on his fingertips until it's washed away by the rain. The lump explains the violent headache. His head hurts so much he can hardly see. The ocean is too loud, crashing on the rocks nearby. Bass looks around. He has washed up in a little cove. It's not much more than a hollow carved out of a rocky cliff face. Rain splashes down his face, and suddenly Bass is so thirsty he can't think about anything else. He holds his hands out and licks the rainwater out of his palms as fast as he can. It's not until he's drunk three full handfuls of water that he really remembers how he got here.

"Rosie!" It's not a good shout, more of a broken cough. He tries again. "Rosie!" he yells, stumbling to his knees. His legs are sliced and bloody. His shorts have protected him from the knees up, but the skin on the rest of his right leg is shredded. Must have washed over the rocks. It looks like someone has gone at him with a cheese grater. Once he sees the injuries, his brain seems to process that they hurt. The pain is breathtaking. But there's no time for that. Rosie could be on the rocks or still in the water. Who knows how long he's been here! He has to look for her.

Staggering upright, he half crawls, half walks out onto the slick rocks surrounding him. It looks like he's on a rocky outcrop sticking out from the edge of a larger island. He can't tell which one, but it doesn't look like home. The rain makes it hard to see.

Where he's standing now, the rocks are worn smooth. The ocean pounds up between two large rocks farther out, making a kind of channel. On his left are large, lumpy rocks covered in mussels and barnacles. To his right the cliff juts into the water, blocking off access to any sort of beach or place to walk. He can't go right, so left it is.

Bass is honestly shocked that he's on his feet at all. His toes are bruised and swollen. Though his right leg is a mess of cuts and grazes, his left leg isn't too bad. A broad scrape over his knee is the worst of it. The life jacket protected his upper body well. There are rips in the fabric, and one of the straps has completely torn free. If he hadn't been wearing the life jacket, he definitely would have died. His hands hurt from being in the cold water, but they work okay—he can open and close them. He's so cold his teeth are chattering noisily, and his whole body shivers as he walks. He needs to get warm. Fast. But first he has to find Rosie.

He stumbles down the rocks, as close to the surging water as he dares. He peers left and right, looking for anything out of place. There's nothing. Just endless gray ocean and rocks everywhere.

"Rosie!" he yells again. The word is lost in the wind. "Rosie!" His strength gives out, and he has to stop to lean against a large rock. "Rosie." It's only a whisper this time. The burst of adrenaline he got when he realized he had survived has faded, leaving him weak and shivering. Something moves by his foot and startles him, but it's only a crab. He watches the small creature race over the rocks. Tears burn his eyes and spill over. The small shelter of an overhang keeps the rain off his face.

He sees something move in the shadow where the crab was. Something twitches and opens like a massive spider. For a moment Bass is horrified, and then his eyes focus properly. It's a hand. Rosie's hand.

Chapter Five

Bass makes it to Rosie's side in a second. He doesn't even notice his knee start to seep blood again as he lands on it. A pool of red spreads out on the wet rock as he grabs Rosie by her life jacket. Her eyes are open. They land on Bass, and her eyelids flutter.

"I thought you were dead," Bass says. He's crying again.

"Not…not yet," Rosie says. Her voice is scratchy and sounds painful.

"Are you hurt?" Bass asks, running his hands down Rosie's arms and legs the way he was shown at school. He's never been more grateful for gym class and basic first-aid training. He can't feel anything major broken. Everything seems like it's where it should be.

"Not sure," Rosie says. She's ash pale under her brown skin. Her short hair is tangled and knotted. There's a strand of seaweed draped over her ear. Bass picks it off carefully and helps her sit up. She groans in pain. Leaning against the rock, shoulder to shoulder, Bass starts to laugh.

"We should be dead!" he says. He can't believe they're both here, alive. No major life-threatening injuries. He sticks his shaking hand out into the downpour again, filling it with water. He slurps it down, still thirsty. After a moment Rosie copies him and drinks her fill.

"Still could die. Gotta get warm," she says, and Bass remembers how cold he is. He can barely feel his feet. He and Rosie don't have clothes or towels or anything dry. It's still pouring rain. To get dry they're going to need a fire. Hoping against hope, Bass tries to wriggle his fingers into the pocket of his wet shorts. He can feel the lump of his lighter pressing against his hip. He struggles to pull it clear. His hands are shaking too much to turn the wheel. It's soaked anyway, full of water—when he finally manages it, there's no spark or flame. His excitement drains away, replaced by anger.

"Stupid piece of shit!" He almost throws it into the sea but stops himself at the last second. Maybe it will dry out.

"No good?" Rosie pulls herself to her feet, looking as tired as Bass feels.

"Wet," Bass replies, too angry to say any more.

"Well, everything's wet. Let's try to find a drier spot and some dry wood. Having a lighter won't help if there's nothing to burn," Rosie says. She sounds pretty calm, but Bass can see the tense set of her jaw.

There's nothing else to be done though. His life jacket makes moving difficult, but the wind cutting through his shorts convinces him to keep it on. At least the jacket's holding in some of his body heat. The tiny bit he has. Together, he and Rosie inch deeper under the overhang of rock. It's beautiful, in a we-might-die-here kind of way. The rock looks like liquid. It drips down in a curve that provides some shelter from the wind and spray. It's sandy gray like the rocks by Bass's house, but he's never seen a hollowed-out place like this. It might be spooky on a normal day, but right now it's shelter. It's probably only four yards deep, but there's enough space for them both, and a fire—if they can make one.

Rosie stumbles ahead, also barefoot. She has her own share of cuts and scrapes on her strong legs.

There's blood crusted on the back of her ear. Bass's stomach churns at the sight of her injuries. Even though he didn't create the storm or take them out in the boat, somehow it feels like this is his fault. As though if he were a better sailor, a better person, this wouldn't have happened. Rosie turns and gives him a weak grin. "Wood."

She's right—there's driftwood. Most of it is damp, washed up in the storm. But some of it is older. It must have been here since before the rain. A crevice like this catches lots of floating debris. Some of it gets stuck. Slumping down, Bass starts pulling dry bits of wood and seaweed together, making a small pile with Rosie's help.

Bass picks up the lighter and flicks the wheel again. Nothing happens. No spark. No joy. No fire. When he turns the lighter upside down, water trickles out. A faint memory hits him out of nowhere. Camping with his dad. The lighter wet from being dropped in a puddle. His dad rubbing the lighter, upside down, across the sole of his boot. Again and again until the lighter sparked. Bass shakes with excitement instead of cold. "I think I know how to dry it!" He's not wearing shoes, so instead he grabs a dryish piece of driftwood. Turning the lighter upside down, he frantically runs the wheel over the wood. His hands are stupid with cold, but they can just manage this. He jerks the flint against the wood, over and over. For what feels like forever, nothing happens.

He's about to give up when the hopeless clicking noise changes slightly. He looks closer on his next try, and his heart swells. A faint spark!

"It's working!" Rosie says, excited. She huddles closer. The tiny bit of warmth coming off her feels so good that Bass leans back. Resting the wood on his thigh for support, he works the lighter a few more times until a spark appears every time.

Holding his breath, he turns the lighter over and presses the wheel down with his thumb.

Spark...flame! With shaking hands, he keeps the gas button depressed and lowers the tiny flame to their pile of wood and seaweed. The heat from the lighter is so glorious, he wants to hold it up to his other hand, but they might only get one shot at this. Holding his breath, he lets the small flame lick the dry, fluffy seaweed. It sizzles but doesn't catch. The lighter sputters and goes out.

Chapter Six

"Shit!" Bass says. He's so cold it's getting hard to think. "C'mon, come on!" He's not sure how many more tries he has in him. Rosie's shaking even harder than he is. An image of them being found dead next to an unlit fire pops into his head. *NO! You will not die of cold after surviving that storm.* His inner voice has never sounded so confident. Bass puts the lighter down on his chunk of wood and brings his hands up to his mouth. He blows air into them. His breath is not exactly warm, but it's warmer than his fingers. Again and again he puffs his breath into his hands, trying to make them work properly.

"Do you want me to try?" Rosie asks through rattling teeth.

"No, I got this. Get ready to feed it," Bass says. He wants to succeed so badly he can taste it. He takes one last breath and blows it into his hands. Then he snatches up the lighter.

Once, twice, three times he clicks it, and the spark finally catches. He can't believe his dad's trail trick has worked. He can't believe *he* made his dad's trail trick work. Slowly, to protect the small flame, Bass guides the lighter back to the pile of seaweed and tiny pieces of wood.

Rosie uses a thin stick to make a space under the seaweed, and Bass holds the lighter as close as he dares. If he puts the flame out against the kindling, they might lose their last chance.

Bass can only see the flame. Everything in him narrows to concentrate on the spark of hope. The warmth licks at his thumb. The seaweed catches, glows orange. Heat, almost too hot to bear against his chilled skin. He holds on, trying as hard as he can to keep his hand still. If he shakes too hard, the wind might destroy their baby fire. The flame grows, covering the smallest twigs Rosie's pushing closer. They've built their tiny fire in behind a rock, where the wind can hardly reach it. A stick cracks, throwing up sparks. Bass doesn't dare stop holding the lighter, but it's too hot. He can't hold it anymore. Wincing, he yanks his hand back. Breath frozen in his chest, he watches. The flame sputters. Grows. Bass uses his unscorched hand to move some more little twigs into the baby blaze.

"Oh my god, Bass," Rosie says, "you did it. Fire." She sounds so happy Bass can't help but laugh a little.

"Fire," he agrees.

Together they nurse the small flames until larger sticks will catch. When one the size of Bass's wrist ignites, he relaxes against the rock wall. He looks at Rosie. "We made fire! I feel like...an explorer or a caveman...cave*person*...who just discovered fire for the first time."

"With a lighter." Rosie rubs her hands up and down her arms. It's still unbearably cold everywhere that isn't an inch from the fire. She starts to pull off her life jacket, fumbling with the zipper. It takes her four tries, but eventually she gets it. She shrugs out of the heavy, wet material. She grins at Bass, huddling close to the fire. "We're going to be okay."

Bass tries to squash the voice that reminds him they have no boat, no one knows where they are, and the storm is still raging. At least their sheltering place looks like it doesn't get submerged at high tide. They'll probably die of hunger. Or thirst, if the rain stops.

"Bass." Rosie moves closer to him. Her shoulder pushes up against his shoulder. Automatically Bass lifts his arm so she can cuddle in, but she pulls away. "Eww," she says.

Bass blinks, shocked and a little hurt. He's sure he doesn't smell great, but they are shipwrecked, after all. *Eww* seems pretty harsh. He blinks at her, but Rosie just grabs the zipper and tugs his life jacket off. He manages to help a bit, but he's still confused.

"Wet. Cold. I want to hold you, not a gross, sodden piece of foam or whatever." Rosie pushes his jacket into the gap between their fire rock and another rock. Immediately Bass feels warmer. The heat reflects back, pooling in their little "cave." It's almost like sliding into a warm bath.

"Whoa," Bass says. *Eloquent as ever.*

Rosie grins smugly and settles back against him. He can feel the slight warmth of her face through his soaked T-shirt and the strips of trans tape holding his chest flat. His back is against the cold rock, leeching his heat. But the fire is warm in front of him and on his stretched-out legs. Rosie is warm under his arm. Bass's heartbeat feels like it's echoing in the small space. His head sags until it's resting on Rosie's. His eyes keep closing. Every time he forces them open, the fire looks smaller. He can't bring himself to care. It's so warm, and he's so tired. His whole body hurts. It's okay if he just rests for a minute, right?

The next time Bass opens his eyes, the fire is out.

Chapter Seven

Bass jerks fully awake. Rosie's head slips, and she moans in complaint.

"Shh. Bad pillow," she says, snuggling back into Bass.

"Rosie! Rosie, the fire's gone out!" Bass shakes her shoulder, trying to get her properly awake.

"That's okay," Rosie mumbles. "We can call Smokey the Bear."

As cute as her sleepy rambling is, Bass shakes her harder. "Rosie, wake up!"

"What?" Rosie sits up, her hair sticking out wildly from her head. As soon as her eyes are open, she freezes. "Oh, fuck me."

The temperature in their little hideaway is already dropping. The warm air still coming from the smoking ends of the wood in the fire is quickly getting snatched away by the wind.

Rosie makes a sound that could be a laugh or a sob. Or both. "We fell asleep." Their clothes are still damp. No longer dripping, but wet enough that Bass can feel his body heat being pulled out of him. He clenches his teeth so they won't chatter.

"I'll light it again." He fumbles in his clammy shorts pocket, where he'd tucked the lighter safely away, and pulls it out. Hastily they both grope around their small space for fuel.

It's fully dark now. Night fell as they slept, exhausted from their battle with the ocean. But there are no stars or a moon to provide light, and their shelter is almost pitch black. "I can't find any dry seaweed," Bass says. His tone sounds high and panicked, and he makes an effort to lower it. Testosterone has made his voice deeper, but it's still much more feminine than he feels comfortable with. He tries to ignore the sudden dysphoria—that's the word his counsellor uses for 'the distress that comes from conflict between his gender identity and his biological sex'—so he can focus. This is not the best time to be having a trans identity crisis. Shipwrecked panic, on the other hand? Stranded panic? Perfect time for those.

"Same. It's all damp. Must have soaked up the water from our life jackets." Rosie takes a deep breath. "We can't stay here without a fire."

"It's so cold," Bass says. "But it's also super dark, and we're on some random rocks. Where could we go? We might not be able to find better shelter."

"We don't need better shelter," Rosie says grimly. "We need to find people. No one's looking for us out here. They won't send the coast guard unless they realize we've got Old Jack's boat, which they won't. The only way they'd find out is if someone pulled the tarp up and saw that it's gone. But in a storm like this, no way would they think anyone had been foolish enough to take the boat. So we're on our own."

Rosie pauses for a moment. Bass can tell she is really, really scared. "I can barely feel my feet, Bass," she continues. "Our fire's dead, and even if we get another one started, we've used almost all the dry sticks, so how long would it last? We don't have any food. But we got some sleep. We should try to get to safety now, while we still can. For all we know, we're just around the corner from someone's dock."

Bass looks out the "door" of their shelter. The outside world is a slightly lighter shade of black than the inside of their cave. The wind is still whipping the water into whitecaps that boil up the rocks, but they're smaller now. The rain also appears to have died down a bit. "I don't know, Rosie," he says.

The cave feels safer than the unknown, even if it is cold. Every part of Bass's body feels bruised from the wicked waves and rocks. He's not sure he'll be able to walk far, barefoot and injured.

Rosie sighs and puts her hand on the back of Bass's neck. He leans into the contact, craving the comfort. "I don't know either," she says softly. "But I think we have to try."

"Okay. And besides, I don't have any better ideas." Bass uses a handy rock to lever himself to his feet. He winces when he puts weight on his scraped-up leg. "Can we stick together though?" he asks, suddenly afraid she'll suggest going in two different directions. The only thing worse than this whole situation would be being in it alone.

He can hear the tiny grin in her voice when she replies.

"Yes, please." She slides her hand down from his shoulder to weave their fingers together.

Bass straightens, feeling stronger and braver than he has done all day.

"We got this," he tells her, squeezing her hand gently.

"All right, let's dip," she replies.

They head out into the night. The light rain trickles down Bass's neck in cold, unpleasant streams. They step over the worn, smooth rocks, out of their safe haven. Outside it's brighter, easier to see than Bass expected. The clouds are still thick overhead, but higher than they were earlier. They hang heavy over the angry ocean, but the storm is passing. It makes Bass more confident as they make their way over the rocks.

Their shelter is little more than a deep groove in the cliff face. Its curving sides are smooth. It's almost as if an enormous air bubble popped in liquid rock, leaving a shallow cave. Above the cave, the cliff continues. The sandstone alternates between smooth and rough. The track they're walking on narrows. It gets smaller and smaller, until they can no longer walk side by side. Still holding Bass's hand, Rosie takes the lead. They've only gone about twenty yards from their cave when they encounter a huge gush of water rushing up over the rocks, blocking their way. They can't go any farther. The other direction from the cave looked much harder, but they turn back and retrace their steps.

It becomes clear almost immediately that they won't be able to get out of the cove that way either.

They're trapped.

Chapter Eight

*So this is it. This is how you die. Wet on a rock.
Who do you think will go first? You're bigger, but
you're both lucky enough to be carrying some extra
weight. You'd probably have died in the water if
you weren't. The layers of fat kept you warm. But
drowning would have been quick, at least. And it
would be over now. Instead of this, waiting to slowly
die of hypothermia.*

"I think we can do it," Rosie says, jarring Bass out of his anxious thoughts.

"Do what?" Bass asks. He follows her gaze. She's looking up at the cliff face. It's not absurdly tall, but it's tall enough to prevent a view of the rest of whatever island they're on. At the very top, Bass can see the bony outline of trees. There are dozens of thick horizontal bands across the cliff face, like a giant has made an extremely fancy cake.

"Climb it." Rosie turns to face Bass and points. "Look, there's a way past the overhang." She traces the line in the air, demonstrating what she means.

Bass squints. "Rosie...how the hell do you think I'm going to climb a cliff? I don't even have basic climbing skills!" Bass often feels like a bear. Sort of soft, big and lumbering. He knows bears can climb amazingly well, but this is definitely not a skill set he shares with that creature. The only time he's ever braved climbing, and it was just a tree, was almost ten years ago. That adventure ended in tears and the arrival of the fire department.

"I'll help you," Rosie says. She also snuggles back in under his arm, using his body to block the wind. Bass doesn't mind at all. He'd much rather cuddle with Rosie than attempt to climb this stupid cliff. He wraps his arms around her and runs his palm up and down her shoulder.

"You can just follow me, put your hands where I do. It's not that high. We can make it!" Rosie says, her voice muffled with her nose pressed into his collarbone. There's a spot of warmth spreading from where her lips are brushing Bass's cold skin. It feels almost like a tiny burn.

"I can't do that, Rosie." Bass shakes his head. "There's no way. I'll just slow you down. I'd probably fall, and then what would you do? You should go without me. Try and find help. I can boost you and then stand under you in case you fall. You know, I'll be softer to land on than the rocks."

Rosie giggles. "Way softer."

"Way, way softer." Bass kisses her forehead and then blinks, surprised by his action. This morning he never would have dared to be so bold, but that seems foolish now. Rosie looks up at him, her eyes big and bright in the gloom. It seems like they're catching every sparkle of light available, glinting at him. Bass stops feeling cold. Rosie tilts her chin in an unmistakable invitation, and Bass gets warm deep in his belly. When he leans down to kiss her, she grabs a handful of his wet shirt to hold him close. Their lips meet, clumsy and cold, bumping together. Their noses catch, and they shift to get a better angle. The kiss isn't long, isn't especially deep or passionate, but it's the best kiss Bass has ever shared. They both pull back at the same time, warm breath brushing over each other's cheeks. Bass feels like he's blushing. And he also feels like he actually could climb that cliff.

Rosie spreads her hands out and smooths his T-shirt back into place. "So. Climbing." She sounds a little dazed.

"Climbing," Bass agrees.

They make their way back to where the cliff face curves in, forming their previous shelter. Bass is kind of glad his feet are too cold to feel much. At this point he has stubbed his toes, walked on something sharp or caught his foot on a rock dozens of times.

Looking at the cliff up close makes Bass change his mind. He'd struggle to climb it with a ladder. There's no possible way he'd make it more than five feet up.

"I'm sorry, Rosie. I just don't think I can do it. You're going to have to go without me."

Honestly, he can't really see how Rosie can do it either. He can just barely make out some fist-sized dents in the wall of rock, but they all seem to have sharp edges. Maybe she could grab them with her hands, but how could she stand in them without cutting her feet? She was barefoot when he found her, presumably having kicked her shoes off in the water like he did. He frowns up at the imposing cliff. "You really think you can climb this, Rosie? What if the other side is just more of the same?"

Rosie leans her head on his shoulder. "Well, I figure there's a decent chance we're on one of the headlands sticking off the island. For all we know, there's a house just at the top of the cliff. And if there's not…well…there's a better chance someone will see me up there."

"You should take the lighter." Bass grabs it and tries to press it into her hands. "You should be able to find something dry up there in the trees, and maybe you can make a signal fire. Or at least get dry."

Rosie purses her lips like she wants to disagree, then takes the lighter. "Signal fire. Great idea. Someone will see it."

She leans up to press her mouth against Bass's. It's just a quick peck, but it makes his heart thud in his ears. His eyes are still closed when she pulls back, but he opens them when he hears her chuckle.

"Okay, let's do this!" Bass quickly moves to the cliff and leans his back against it. He braces his hands together across his less injured thigh. "Don't be afraid to step on my head," he adds, grinning at her.

"What a gentleman," Rosie teases. Then she moves closer and places her hands on his shoulders. "I'll get help, Bass, and I'll be back soon."

"Counting on it." Bass tries to sound brave.

Rosie lifts her leg, puts her foot in his cupped hands and thrusts upward. She uses her hands on his shoulders to push herself up, and then all her weight is in Bass's cold, bruised hands. She's heavy, but the cliff is solid behind him. and he plants himself like a tree. He imagines roots going deep and strong into the rock below him. Even when Rosie kicks him in the face by accident as she moves up his body, he doesn't flinch. Then one foot is on his shoulder, the other on his head, and with a last, violent push, her weight is off him.

He steps back and turns. Watches her reach for the next handhold. He can't make out what she's holding on to. He can barely see her shadowy form going upward. She's climbing confidently though. Her body is close to the cliff face, her limbs moving steadily. She's doing it! She's actually doing it.

Bass claps his hands in excitement—he can't help it. He didn't really think she'd be able to get up this smooth cliff face. But she is! She's over three-quarters of the way now and showing no sign of slowing down. Bass steps back and to the right, keeping himself underneath her. He means what he said. If she falls, landing on him is the best option. Much better than crashing onto the rocks and breaking her skull open. Landing in the water wouldn't be much better.

He tries to stop thinking of worst-case scenarios. He wants to shout out encouraging words, but he's worried he'll distract her, so he keeps his mouth shut. He bites his lip, urging her on silently. *C'mon, Rosie. You got this! You're so awesome. I can't believe you're climbing out of this hellscape. Keep going! You can do it!*

The top of the cliff is a dark line. Rosie's easier to see now against the light blue-black of the sky. *She's almost there. She's so close!* Bass thinks she has a hand over the top of the cliff now.

Something bursts free of the cliff face next to her. A black shadow, screeching. A seagull! It must have been roosting on the rock. Rosie flinches back in surprise and, to Bass's horror, slips.

In slow motion she scrambles for a handhold. Her body arches away from the rock. Her balance is gone. Bass sees what's going to happen. *No no no no no no.*

He dives for her as she drifts away from the safety of the cliff. Time speeds up as she falls toward the rocks waiting below.

Chapter Nine

Rosie starts to scream just before she slams into Bass. Her skull thuds into his outstretched arm. Her shoulder slams him in the center of his chest. It knocks the wind right out of him and sends him sprawling. They land in a heap with a horrible, wet, cracking noise. Rosie takes a deep breath and screams again. The noise is animal-like, violent.

"Oh god oh god oh god, Rosie. Rosie!" Bass frantically tries to move her off him and onto the smooth slope of rock so he can help.

She takes a deep, choking breath. "My leg, my *leg*!" she shrieks.

"Rosie, I'm right here. It's okay. You're okay." Bass tries to keep his voice calm and level as he gently wriggles out from under her. Rosie's crying now, huge, heaving sobs that shake her whole body.

As soon as he can sit up, he sees. Her lower leg is clearly broken. It's resting awkwardly on a rock, the ankle at an angle it shouldn't be. Halfway up her shin the bone is sticking out through the skin. There's blood oozing out, black and wet against the paler skin of her calf.

"Oh shit, oh shit, Rosie." Bass flaps his hands uselessly, trying to decide what to do. His whole brain is frozen—he can't think.

"Bass," she sobs. "It hurts. Oh fuck, it hurts so much."

"Okay, you're going to be okay. Your leg is broken, that's why it hurts, but that's okay!" From somewhere inside him, a calm, cooler person takes over. "Take some deep breaths for me, in and out. I'm going to move your leg. It's going to hurt a hell of a lot, but it needs to be level, okay?" Inside he's white noise and silence. Someone confident moves his hands. "On three, all right? One…" He wraps his fingers gently around her calf. "Two…" He takes hold of her foot with his other hand. "Three." As fast as he can, he moves her leg down off the rock.

Rosie moans in pain, and when he looks up at her face, her eyes are closed. She's passed out. *Good. That's good. It must hurt unbearably. It's better if she's unconscious.* Then he remembers. Rosie was climbing to save them. They're trapped here. Alone. No boat. No food. Only rainwater to drink. No fire. Rosie's skin is freezing, and her face is sweaty and pale.

Fuck.

Okay, first things first. The new, confident inner voice is taking over. *Look at her leg.* Reluctantly he does so. When he moved her foot down to straighten the leg, the bone withdrew into the wound. Her ankle and knee are in line now. *Great! That's awesome. You don't have to pull her leg straight. Next you need to find something to bandage the cut.* The wound is deep. Bass can see the blood still welling out of it. Bandages. *Okay. What do we have?* Life jacket? Too hard to rip. T-shirt? Maybe. Tape! Bass feels thunderstruck. He has tape. Trans tape. The six-inch-wide sticky stuff is a lot like an adhesive bandage. He's sure it will restick. Every time he pulls it off at home, it attaches itself to his clothes, furniture, the soles of his shoes. If he can rip some of his T-shirt up for a pad to cover the open wound, he can tape it in place. It'll be just like a bandage.

He can do this.

Bass strips off his shirt. It's been soaked by the ocean, and now that the rain is easing off, it's drying with crusty white patches. Exposed to the wind, his skin pimples with goose bumps.

The tape is meant for going in the water, so the soaking hasn't ruined it. The tape pulls his chest flat, squashing his breasts. It starts just where the cups of a bra would be and drags his flesh out toward his armpits. The tape passes under each arm and sticks on his shoulder blades, not meeting in the middle. Bass digs his nails under the tape edge closest to his sternum. The tape resists, clinging to his skin. He pulls it clear, rolling it back on itself as best he can like you're supposed to. It still kind of hurts. It may be super-special designer tape for trans masc people who want a flat chest without wearing a full binder, but it's still essentially glued to his skin. When the tape is halfway clear, dangling from one end on his back, Bass realizes he's doing things in the wrong order. He has to prep the splint for the fractured leg first.

He curses and sticks the tape back down, but not firmly.

Rosie's still lying there, not moving. The rain falling down her face makes it look like she's crying. Bass wants to get her under shelter, but he knows he has to strap her leg up as best he can first.

Using his teeth, he tears a little hole along the seam of his T-shirt sleeve. The sleeve comes free with some tugging and cursing. He clambers over the rocks to a deep pool of rainwater and rinses the shirt sleeve out a few times. Then he locates a stick he noticed when Rosie was climbing. It's about a foot long and thick enough to work as a really shitty splint. But it's the best he's got. He runs back over the rocks, his feet slipping and sliding. Somehow he stays upright. His heart is pounding, his breath short, but he doesn't have time to panic. He only has time to do his best.

Rosie hasn't moved.

Bass folds the T-shirt sleeve into a rough pad and lays it as gently as he can on top of her seeping leg injury. Rosie doesn't twitch. Quickly Bass places the splint stick next to her leg and starts yanking the tape off his torso. He's less careful this time, leaving abrasions on his skin, but he doesn't care. Eventually he has a few strips of tape he can use. The longest is around twelve inches. He starts with that one. Easing it under Rosie's leg makes the bleeding pick up. At the sight of the flowing blood, Bass's stomach twists and turns inside him. But he doesn't vomit. His fingers are shaking again as he wraps the tape around Rosie's leg, securing first the improvised fabric pad and then the stick to firmly hold her leg straight. He adds the rest of the tape pieces. When he's finished, Rosie's leg is wrapped in bright purple tape. It looks surprisingly professional to Bass. The bleeding is already seeping through, but much more slowly. The dark spot of blood on the tape doesn't grow bigger than a quarter.

Bass exhales. *Okay. What's next?* Shelter. He has to get Rosie back out of the wind and off the wet and slippery rocks.

Lifting Rosie makes Bass aware of just how bruised and injured he is. He's bigger than Rosie, taller by a couple of inches and broader in the chest and shoulders. But she's not light. It takes him three gut-wrenching tries to scoop her up. Her knees in one elbow, her head in the other. Staggering with his burden, Bass limps back over the rocks to their small sanctuary.

Rosie moans as he lays her down, and her eyelids flicker open. It's getting lighter outside. They've been here all night.

"I'm here, Rosie. I've got you." Bass does his best impression of his mom when he gets hurt. Keeps his voice soothing and calm. He strokes her hair back off Rosie's chilled forehead. "I'm just going to prop your leg up a bit and use the life jacket as a support. I've already bandaged it. Everything's going to be fine."

While he's talking, he pulls the abandoned life jacket toward him. He wishes he had a knife. If he could cut the jacket up, he could use the straps to make a tight, padded support for Rosie's injured leg. As it is, he has to just arrange her leg on the back of it. At least it's padded and keeps the leg more secure. He does his best to wrap the front pieces over her leg and clips the buckles closed as tightly as possible.

"Done. Now, Rosie, I'm going to get help. Just try to rest. I'll be back soon, I promise. Everything's going to be okay."

Chapter Ten

Bass rubs his hands over his face. His stringy, wet hair gets tangled around his fingers, and he swears violently. It feels good to swear, so he does it some more.

"Fuck, fuck, *fuuuuuck!*" he yells at the universe. At the sky for sending the storm, at the ocean for flooding their boat and washing them up. At the stupid rocks that broke Rosie's leg. His yells turn to sobs, until he's crouched down and crying. He holds his knees and rocks back and forth like he did as a baby. As quickly as the tears hit, they vanish. He hiccups, panting for air. *Enough. You don't have time for this. Break down later. Help first.*

The cliff looks even more intimidating in the better light. Bass glares up at it like he can make it smaller if he's angry enough. It doesn't shrink. The trees on the top are easy to see against the gray dawn sky. If only one of them had grown roots down the rocky face. Bass looks in vain for handholds he can use to climb. Rosie's depending on him. He has to get out of here somehow.

He rests his hands in two convenient dents and inhales. He manages to get his left foot wedged into a little crack and pushes up. His ribs scream in protest as he stretches. He reaches out with his right hand and walks his fingers into another dent. Grabs on. Tries to pull himself higher, so he can move his other leg off the ground. As soon as his weight rests entirely on his hands, his grip slips. He thuds back to the ground. Gritting his teeth, he tries again. And again. And again. After his fourth failure to get even three feet off the ground, he gives up.

Tears spring into his eyes, but he wipes them away. He won't break down. Rosie needs to get to a hospital. Bass has stopped the bleeding, but she's still in danger. The cold has already almost killed them. Now she has a broken leg as well. Moving around has warmed Bass up fully for the first time since he hit the water. He rubs his arms with his hands while he thinks. If he can't go up...he'll have to go around.

Bass turns to face the water. The wind may have dropped, but it's still whipping up the waves. Whitecaps roll into the rocks and splash up into the air. Bass tightens his jaw. It's the only way, he tells himself. If there might be a house just over the cliff, there also might be a house just around the rocky corner. Or maybe he can make his way around this jumble of rocks and back onto shore, perhaps walk around the island. He can't climb, that much is clear. And without help Rosie will die. They'll both die if no one happens to come past in a boat and notice them. Unless Bass does something, he'll have to watch Rosie die, and then he'll die too. He can wait around for someone else to save them, or he can do it himself.

Once he's made the decision, there doesn't seem to be any point in putting it off. He ducks back into their cave to grab the second life jacket—the one that isn't being used as a support. He struggles into it and gets the zipper done up. It's a much tighter fit with his chest free, and he loosens the side straps before buckling them up.

"Rosie. Can you hear me?" He leans down over her still form. Her eyes are closed again, but her fingers are twitching.

"Bass?"

Her voice is so weak.

"Yeah. It's me. I just wanted to let you know help is on the way. I have to go and signal them in. We'll be back soon." Bass has to lie. He doesn't want Rosie to know he's going back into the water. She'd tell him not to.

But Rosie doesn't respond, falling back into an uneasy sleep. Bass grits his teeth, fighting tears. He leans down and kisses her forehead gently. She's cold, but there's nothing he can cover her with. But it's light! Light enough to see! Hastily Bass clambers around the rocks and gathers as much dry wood as he can find. Building a little fire isn't so hard this time. He feels like an old hand when he sparks the lighter against the ball of seaweed he's rolled up.

To his relief, it catches without too much difficulty. It's not the same as being able to stay with her, but at least a fire will help keep Rosie warm. The wind can reach into their whole shelter now, with the lifejacket no longer a barrier. But it's the best Bass can do. The fire is sheltered enough, wedged as it is against a rock. It'll burn out soon. There's nothing to be done about that though. He builds it as high as he dares, checks Rosie's leg one last time and then leaves the cave.

Their cave is even less impressive now that he can see it clearly. Bass still feels scared to leave it. Going back into the water feels like the stupidest thing he's ever done. It also feels like the bravest thing he's ever done—and the only choice. Before he sets off, he wedges his bright red T-shirt into a crack in the rock. It's not much, but it might get noticed. If—no, *when* someone comes to find Rosie, this will guide them in. Satisfied with his "flag," he inches over to a smooth rock on the edge of the water. Sitting down on it, he shuffles along until his feet are submerged. It's shockingly cold. So cold it hurts. Bass takes a deep breath and thrusts himself off the rock.

Chapter Eleven

The icy water hits him like a hammer. The shock of it drives the air from his lungs. His head goes under, but his life jacket pulls him back to the surface. Spluttering and coughing, he tries to get his bearings. The waves push him back against the rocks, but his life jacket is enough to protect him from the impact. The water's not quite as rough as he feared. He pushes himself around the rocks, using his hands and shoulders. His hands get grazed by barnacles, sliced by mussel shells, but the cold hides the pain he knows he should feel. Blood streams down the wet rock as he hauls himself along.

The cold is an ache in his teeth, a tightness in his belly. Water splashes up into his face, stinging his sinuses and making it hard to get a full breath. Soon the rocks change. Instead of being smooth and flat, they become rough and jagged. The ocean has tossed them against each other and left a jumble of sharp edges. Bass balls his hands into fists and wraps his arms around his head. He uses his numb feet and legs to push him clear of the dangerous rocks.

A wave grabs him and spins him around. He's thrust under. Pressure keeps pushing down on him, like hands on his shoulders, holding him under. He can't get clear. His lungs feel like they're seizing in his chest. He can't breathe. *He can't breathe.* The fight drains out of him. He can't make it. He was an idiot he was to think he could, to think he could swim to safety and get help. He's nothing but a pathetic fool trying to be a hero. A fool who's about to be a corpse. He can't tell which way is up. Giving in feels peaceful, feels right. He opens his mouth, unable to resist any longer.

Another huge wave hits him in the back. The last bit of air escapes in a flurry of bubbles to the surface, and Bass feels them run over his chin, his neck. He's upside down, trying to swim clear into the bottom of the ocean. With the last of his strength, Bass flips around and pushes off the slippery rock floor. His strong legs catapult him toward the surface, and his life jacket buoys him up. His vision is turning gray at the edges, but then sweet, sweet air breaks over his face. He takes a huge breath. It takes a few more mouthfuls of air before he starts to feel remotely like he can open his eyes. To his shock, he has made it around the protruding headland. The rocks continue to edge right into the ocean, dropping off steeply.

Bass bobs on the surface, trying to keep his head above water. Now he's past the waves rolling onto the outcrop that had blocked their path. It's calmer here, the waves no longer breaking on him. He can finally catch his breath and look around. He doesn't think he'll be able to climb to shore on these sharp and slick rocks. Which means he has no choice but to keep swimming. There's no way he'd make it back past the mini whirlpool that dragged him under. It almost took him down the first time. Mind made up, Bass kicks out again, trying to swim parallel to the shore without getting too close. His body is so bruised he's grateful for the cold. Being numb is better than knowing just how badly those rocks beat him up.

He can't see any signs of life. No convenient boat out fishing in the morning light. No one walking on the shore. He supposes that would have been too much to wish for. *Just let me get to land. Let me find someone who can help Rosie. Let her be okay, please.*

If anything is listening, please keep her safe. There is no answer to his internal prayer. His body feels so tired it's almost all he can do to keep kicking his bare feet in an effort to move along. If the current were fighting him, he'd be helpless. But for once something's going his way. The current whirling around the rocks is pushing him in the direction he wants to go.

Panting and kicking, Bass labors on. His whole life becomes breathe, kick, breathe, kick. *Onto your back to rest for a moment, then breathe, kick, breathe, kick.* He kicks until he can't anymore. He kicks until he's so tired he's just floating, drifting in and out of sleep. If he didn't have a life jacket on, he'd have drowned for sure by now. He's surprised every time he wakes up to a watery splash on his face— surprised he isn't dead. He keeps swimming. He is getting delirious. He starts muttering Dory's mantra from *Finding Nemo*. Just keep swimming, just keep swimming. It helps a little. Even if it means he's losing it.

Suddenly something grabs at him. It has a hold on his life jacket. Bass panics, waving his arms around wildly, trying to free himself.

"Jesus, kid. Relax, will ya? I'm trying to help you," a gruff voice says. "What the heck happened to ya?"

Bass is too exhausted to answer. He feels himself being pulled up and out of the water, onto something hard that rocks back and forth. A boat maybe. Or a canoe. He tries to open his eyes, but everything hurts and the sun is too bright. "Rosie," he says, so quietly he can barely hear himself. "Rosie's on the rocks. Look…" He almost passes out, snatches himself back to reality for another second. "Look for the red shirt."

Chapter Twelve

Things get confusing for a while. There are questions, people prodding Bass. He's roughly stripped out of his life jacket and shorts. He's wrapped in heat. Blankets are tucked around him, deliciously snug. Heat-radiating pads are placed on his belly and feet. He's so exhausted he can't focus properly. He has to tell them about Rosie. Every time he surfaces from the confusion of not-quite dreams, he tries to tell them. "She's on the rocks," he tells them. "She's hurt. Her leg is broken. You have to save her." No matter how many times he says it, they just respond with soothing nonsense.

"Don't worry about that now. Just relax. Just rest," they say. As though he could stop worrying.

He wakes up again in a white room. There's beeping. Some kind of announcement. Distant commentary on a sports event? Baseball game? Bass tries to make sense of things. Everything's blurry, and he can't see properly.

"Bass? Oh my stars, Bass. Can you hear me? It's me! It's Mom." Her voice calms something inside of him, like the ocean was in his belly, waves crashing into his ribs. His mom's voice smooths the waters.

"Mom?" he asks. He sounds so young, so frail. He tries to turn so he can see her, but he's bundled in too many blankets. Before he can wriggle free, his mom is hugging him. She scoops him into her arms, regardless of the fact he's six inches taller than her.

He feels like a baby as she holds him. He cries into her shoulder, getting snot and tears all down her neck. She just rocks him and shushes him like she did when he was little.

"It's okay now, it's okay, my love. You're safe," she whispers in his ear.

"Rosie?" he asks. He has to know. His brain is slow and sticky, but he knows Rosie's in trouble. He left her. Why did he leave her? He's in the hospital, but where is she?

His mom doesn't lie to him. He doesn't lie to her. It was a deal they made when he came out just over a year ago. That they would always try to be honest with each other. Bass had persuaded himself that skipping school and stealing a boat didn't count as lying. He hadn't ever actually said he was going to school, after all. Okay, so that's pushing it. Still, he knows she'll tell him the truth now.

"I'm so sorry, my love," his mom says. Bass's heart drops down through his chest. It sits heavy in his stomach, a rock he can't digest. "They haven't found her yet," his mom continues.

It takes a moment for Bass's brain to catch up. To process her words. *They haven't found her yet.* Not *she's dead* or *she's not there.* Not having found her isn't good, but there's still hope.

"How long has it been since they found me?" Bass asks. Now his voice sounds like an old man's.

His mom checks her watch. It was his dad's, before he died. Just an old, beaten-up Casio, but it makes Bass so happy to see it that his eyes fill with stinging tears again.

"Almost five hours," she tells him. "But they called the coast guard as soon as you told them she was still out there. I'm sure we'll hear something soon."

"I left her." Bass tries to push back his tears by rubbing his eyes. He rubs them so hard it leaves sparkling green confetti in his vision. "I left her there."

"You left her there to get help, kiddo. What else could you do? You were so brave! I'm so proud of you."

She smiles. "But don't get me wrong, mister. I'm also very angry that you skipped school, took a boat and endangered both your lives. But that can wait. Right now I'm just glad you're okay."

Bass smiled weakly. Mister is one his favorite terms of endearment. His mom loves nicknames, and she had to change a lot of them when he came out. Madam immediately became mister, and it makes him feel loved and accepted every time she says it.

"Rosie was so brave." Bass sniffs. "She climbed up the rocks to go for help. She would have made it, too, if a seagull hadn't flown right in her face. But she fell. She broke her leg really bad. The bone was sticking out." He swallows, his stomach turning as he remembers the injury. "I tried to bandage it up, but she was in so much pain. And it was so cold." He's suddenly hit with a realization. "I should go! I should go with the coast guard and show them exactly where we were. Help them find her! My T-shirt could have blown off the rock and into the water or something. They might never find her!"

His mom puts her hand on his shoulder and firmly holds him on the bed. "You're not going anywhere, buddy," she says gently.

"I have to help her, Mom," Bass says, putting his hand over hers. They're almost the same size, his just slightly bigger. The difference is exaggerated by the white gauze wrapped around two of his fingers and the small bandages stuck all over his skin.

"You did help her," his mom insisted. "You got to safety and sent out the coast guard. They are trained to find people in situations like this. You have to trust them to do their jobs. You're in the hospital. You have hypothermia. The doctors and I agree. You're not going anywhere."

"I'll never forgive myself if she dies." Bass slumps down into the bed. He wants nothing more than to roll over on his side and curl up in a ball. He's too wedged in by blankets, so he has to settle for turning his face away from his mom. Tears roll down his cheeks.

"And I'd never forgive myself if anything happened to you." His mom strokes his head with a gentle hand.

"I feel fine!" Bass insists. He knows it's a losing battle, but he has to try.

"You just woke up after being unconscious for hours, after almost drowning. You may have a mild concussion, not to mentioning being covered in cuts and bruises. And you're on an IV." His mom is using her "don't argue with me" voice now.

Bass knows his bottom lip is sticking out like a sulky toddler's, but he can't help it. Sullenly he closes his eyes. "I'm tired." He is, but mostly he's frustrated and angry.

His mom's voice is soft when she replies, "Go to sleep, kiddo. Maybe when you wake up there'll be good news."

Chapter Thirteen

"Bass, sweetie. Bass, wake up," a voice says.

"I'm sick. I don't want to go to school," Bass replies. His head hurts and his belly aches. His nose is stuffed up and sore, and his throat hurts.

"Baby, Rosie's been brought in." It's his mom, Bass realizes. It all comes back. He's in the hospital. Rosie!

He sits up too fast, getting tangled in the soft pink blankets. Groaning, he tries to free himself. "Rosie!

She's alive?" He flinches as the IV needle in the back of his hand gets caught on something.

"Alive and kicking," his mom says, helping him sort out the knot of fabric wrapped around his arm. "They brought her in right after you did a grumpy nap. You've been asleep almost six hours."

Bass can't help but laugh. A grumpy nap is what he used to take when he was a kid. "She's okay?" he asks. The pain in his body is faded now. He's stiff, but in a distant way. Painkillers, he assumes.

"She's going to be okay. They needed to operate on her leg, but she's out of surgery now and recovering. They said you can go and see her, if you want."

"Yes! Yes, I want," Bass replies eagerly. He can't quite believe that Rosie is here, that they found her and she's alive. He has to see her to know it's real.

"Okay, kiddo. I'll get a nurse." His mom tugs his ear gently before getting up and leaving the room.

While she's gone, Bass looks around properly for the first time. He's by the window, in a curtained-off section he assumes means he's sharing a room. Outside the window he can see mountains and houses. It looks like home. Bass sniffs as he thinks about how close he came to losing all this. To dying. To leaving his mom behind on her own. He can't believe he's here, safe, and Rosie is too. It feels like a gift.

The nurse bustles in with a wheelchair, and Bass swiftly wipes his eyes. "Good morning, Bass. You look like you're feeling a bit better!" She parks the wheelchair and comes over to his bed. Bass submits to her poking and prodding for a few minutes, and then she stands back with a smile. "Everything looks good. I hear you want to go and visit your friend."

Bass's mom leans in the doorway, an affectionate look on her face. Bass looks at her and shrugs a shoulder. "My girlfriend," he says. It feels right when he says it. He should probably talk to Rosie about it, once she's up for it, but he thinks he knows what she'll say. Going through what they did together—

91

it was a very emotional first date, to say the least. His mom scrunches her nose up at him. It's her "you're so cute" face. Bass pokes his tongue out at her.

"Your girlfriend, right," the nurse says in a friendly voice. "Let's get you into this wheelchair and go see her then. We'll have to take your IV along for the ride."

Bass opens his mouth to argue that he doesn't need a wheelchair, but catches his mom's raised eyebrow and thinks better of it. It takes them a few minutes to get him settled in the chair, holding on to his IV pole, and then they set off.

The hospital isn't busy. Bass's mom seems to sense that he needs some quiet on the way. Which is good, because Bass is all tongue-tied thinking of Rosie. Wondering if her leg is going to be okay, if she'll be able to do the hammer throw again. If she'll hate him for leaving her there, injured and scared. His throat gets tighter and tighter the closer they get to her room.

"She's just in here," the nurse tells him, slowing the wheelchair and pointing to a ward doorway. "I'll pop in to see if she's awake."

"Are her mom and dad there?" Bass asks his mom.

"Yes, they got here before she was brought in. We've already gotten acquainted. Should I tell them that Rosie's your girlfriend?" his mom teases.

"Mom!" Bass says quietly. "Don't you dare."

"I'm just teasing." His mom leans down and kisses his head. "But you have nothing to worry about. They're going to love you."

"Once they get to know me, maybe." Bass is quite aware that he doesn't make the best first impression. His multicolored hair, his awkwardness, not to mention the whole trans thing...those things usually take a while for people to get their heads around.

His mom snorts and pushes him into the room when the nurse signals for them to come in.

"Hi again, Sheila and Tom. This is Bass. Bass, these are Rosie's parents, Sheila and Tom." Sheila is short and round, like Rosie herself, but Tom is who Rosie gets her features from. He smiles at Bass, showing the same kind of dimples Rosie has.

"Hi, Bass. It's good to see you up and about. How're you feeling?" Rosie's dad asks, coming around the bed to shake Bass's hand. He looks pale and tired, but happy.

"I'm okay," Bass replies, surprised by the friendly gesture. He doesn't want to be rude, so he tries to restrain himself from climbing out of his wheelchair to get a look at Rosie. He can barely see her under all the blankets. Her leg is out, in a cast and propped up on a device.

"Bass?" a croaky voice asks.

His heart swells in his chest. "Rosie," he whispers.

Bass's mom wheels him over to the other side of the bed. Rosie looks up at him. Her huge dark eyes are bloodshot. There are plum-colored bruises underneath both of them. Her lips are cracked and dry. Bass has never seen her look more beautiful.

"You made me a fire," she says. Her voice is unsteady. She reaches out a bruised hand, and instinctively Bass takes it. He rests their joined hands on the blanket near her hip.

"Yeah. And I left you there." He doesn't mean to say that, but it bursts out.

"You had to," Rosie says. She's obviously exhausted, and there's a haunted look on her face that Bass doesn't like. But it fades away when she smiles and flashes her dimples. "You saved us."

Bass grins properly for the first time since the storm broke.

"Yeah, I guess I did."

NOW WHAT? Read on for an excerpt from *Blood Sport*

SOMEBODY KNOWS SOMETHING.

Jason infiltrates a boxing gym in search of the truth about his sister's mysterious death.

Chapter One

Jason's hands won't stop shaking. He clenches his fists, his sister's silver ring digging into his palm, but they keep shaking. He bursts into tears the second the door finally closes.

He can hear the footsteps of the police officer walking away. The same one who came six weeks ago to inform him of his sister's death.

Door closed and case closed. In front of Jason, on the sad, small bed in the sad, small room, is everything Becca left behind. Two boxes—a whole life—and Jason's hope for a future. He is about to age out of the foster-care system. In four months, when he turns eighteen, he'll be booted out of the group home. Maybe onto the street. Becca was supposed to be here. Becca was supposed to take care of him. But all that's left of Becca are these two boxes.

It's hard to breathe. His binder must be too tight. His chest feels like it's collapsing. It takes him three tries to get his shirt off. He pulls off the material crushing his breasts down flat and throws it on the old blanket on the bed. He feels better, but barely.

Two years on testosterone, male hormones, has changed Jason. It's made his shoulders wider, his jaw bigger and his body hairier. But without a shirt, it is easy to see what he is. A transgender guy. Someone in danger. The staff at the group home know, of course. They take him to get his shots and see his doctors. But if any of the other kids found out, Jason would be in for a world of hurt.

He stands in the middle of the room, his mind full of pain and fear. He feels like he's dying. He can't breathe at all.

After a while the panic attack fades. As he calms down he realizes he's half-naked. It would be *so* bad if someone walked in right now. Running to the bed, he grabs his binder. The door bangs open before he can put it back on.

Panicking, Jason drops the binder and grabs his shirt. If anyone sees his chest, they'll know what he has been hiding. He pulls the shirt over his head, his back still to the door. He prays for his strong shoulders to help him pass. For whoever it is to see just a boy.

"Yo, Jase, saw the pigs came by again. Did they solve your sister's murder yet?" The thick voice can only belong to Derek. Jason hates Derek. The guy is built like a monster and has a personality to match.

It takes everything Jason has in him to sound normal. "Not yet." Ever since he'd yelled at the care worker that his sister couldn't have overdosed, that she never did drugs, not *ever*, the other teens at the care home like to tease him about it. Especially Derek.

Jason's whole body shivers as he wonders whether Derek wants to fight again. Jason's ribs are still bruised from last time. If he stays facing away, his back is open to possible danger. If he turns around, Derek might see his chest under his shirt.

To his relief, Derek just snorts and bangs back out into the hallway. Jason waits until the door shuts behind him and then rushes to it. He kicks the door stopper tightly into place. It's dangerous. In case there's a fire. He's not supposed to have it. They've taken four off him already, but it's the only way he can breathe in this place.

Safely locked in, Jason walks slowly back to the bed. His whole body feels like it's full of rocks. What is he going to do without Becca? How can this be his life now?

Dropping down on the bed, he knocks one of the boxes over. It tips sideways, spilling its contents onto the blankets.

The copy of Sherlock Holmes that falls out makes him gasp. It was their dad's, the collected stories. When he'd lost his job and started drinking, he'd started selling most of his first editions. But Becca had taken this one. First it had been in her bedroom, on the shelf by her bed. Then, after she moved out, it was on display in her apartment, which Jason was going to move into once he left the group home. Part of their plan.

The book is light brown, with gold leaf on the leather cover and gold-edged pages. Becca has read it so often that the creamy cover is dirty. He reaches out to put the book back in the box. He can't face looking through the pieces of her life. But as he picks up the book he realizes there's something wrong.

The page edges aren't shiny like they should be. They are dull and brown, no gold in sight. Curious, he picks up the book. He runs his finger down the spine. The cover feels weird in his hand.

He opens the book. As soon as he does, he can see what's wrong. The pages aren't pages at all. The cover of the book has been stuck onto a box. Sherlock Holmes's adventures aren't anywhere to be seen. There are no pages inside. No stories. Instead there are dozens of newspaper clippings.

Missing girls. Reports of missing girls from the Downtown Eastside. Dating back more than two years. The one with the oldest report has a face he vaguely recognizes. Anna Kerov, one of Becca's friends from work. She was a cocktail server, like Becca. Reported missing in 2017.

Why did his sister have these? Why was she collecting, and hiding, reports of missing girls? Jason's heart is beating too fast. His hands are shaking again. Becca must have been mixed up in something bad. Why else would she have this stuff?

Under the clippings there's something else. A flat white square. Not paper. Thicker. It is wedged into the corners of the box, and it takes a bit of effort to wiggle it free.

It's a Polaroid photo. A shot of a street. Two dark figures standing under a neon sign. Even with two letters blown out, Jason can see that it should say *Ray's Place*. A pair of red boxing gloves next to the name look like they probably flashed on and off.

What does this all mean? A photo of a boxing gym, in a box full of newspaper articles about missing girls. And now Becca is dead. Jason is more sure than ever that she didn't overdose.

His hand tightens around the photograph and crushes it into a ball.